California

California

Ray Banks

CRIME EXPRESS

California
by Ray Banks

Published in 2011 by Crime Express
Crime Express is an imprint of
Five Leaves Publications,
PO Box 8786, Nottingham NG1 9AW
www.fiveleaves.co.uk

ISBN: 978 1 907869 07 5

© Ray Banks, 2011

Crime Express 9

Five Leaves acknowledges financial support
from Arts Council England

Five Leaves is represented by Turnaround
and distributed by Central Books.

Cover design: Gavin Morris

Typeset and design;
Four Sheets Design and Print

Printed by Imprint Digital in Great Britain

ABERDEENSHIRE LIBRARY & INFO SERV	
3055687	
Bertrams	18/10/2011
LF	£4.99

1.

When he thought about it, like, Shuggie Boyle reckoned he'd been through some names in his time.

First there was Kevin Munroe, who'd been this close to an aggravated assault pinch before he managed to rabbit; George Cooper, who'd been nabbed fare dodging on the Edinburgh-Glasgow line; Jimmy Fogarty shoplifted a pair of Adidas Kicks back when they were still worth a fence; and Brian Cole punted knock-off Lamberts and litre bottles of Bacardi to half the shipyards. All the names were nice and forgettable. All of them suited his face, which was also nice and forgettable. So he had imagination. He could've made up another name for the pensioner sat next to him, but he didn't. Didn't even use his court name, either — it was all informal, all "tell you what, just call us Shugs if it makes you feel better, eh?"

Truth be told, he didn't know why he said it. The more he thought about it, the more his head hurt. It was a fucking mug's game using his real name and he should've known better, but there was something about the old bloke that reminded him of his Granda. Not that the pensioner looked anything like his Granda, but there was a poppy in his buttonhole, a strength despite the shakes, a bit of bolsh in there. Also, there was the smell of booze on him.

Didn't matter. Whatever it was, it got Shug's yap going.

"I know this isn't ideal for you," he said, "and I know you're sitting there, probably think you're being punished for something, eh?" Shug tapped his head, kept his eyes on the road. "Brain's ticking over, you're thinking about alternative universes. Like if you hadn't stopped at that red light that we both know was a smidge off of green, you would've got away. Thing is, mind, you didn't. I got in, and here we are and all that, and it's ancient history. What's done is done. No point dwelling on the past, because it won't change the present, will it?"

Shug glanced at the old man. According to his driving licence, his name was Charlie Brown. Shug thought it was funny. The old man didn't. Kept that same thin face on him the whole time, staring straight ahead.

"D'you understand what I'm talking about, Charlie?"

Nothing.

Shug nodded to himself. "Okay, alright, fine. I understand, you're having a hard time ... *assimilating* what's happening. That's understandable. Your brain's all closed up. But you'll come round. You'll open up." He slapped Charlie's knee. "Don't you worry, everything'll be fine. All I'm saying is there's no point in blaming yourself for what happened. It's not your fault. You weren't to know. It all happened too quickly for you to react. And you know what, you're better off *not* reacting, you get me? Because I'm a man with a goal, and I will reach that goal no matter what. So you should *thank* yourself, y'know, pat yourself on the back for not doing anything stupid like fight back. Because if you had, I might've had to hurt you, and we don't want it to get to that, do we?"

Charlie looked at him. Milky blue eyes. His mouth moved like he was grinding his dentures.

"Anyway, I'm sorry for nicking your car, Charlie. I'm not daft: this is probably your last shot at independence, this motor. People telling you you can't drive because you've got too many miles on the clock yourself. Bastards to a man, Charlie. Don't let them get to you. You're a better man than they know. And because you are, here's what I'm going to do: I'm going to do you a favour."

Shug waited for a reaction. He didn't get one.

"Okay," he said. "This car. I hate to be the one to break it to you, but she's not long for this world. So what I'm going to do for you — when I drop you off, the first thing you should do is call it in stolen. Then, what I'm going to do is take this off somewhere and put her out of her misery, what d'you say? It's win-win. I get a ride, you get a new motor out of your insurance. You've got comp, haven't you? That's how it works, doesn't it? Can't say I ever had insurance, myself."

Charlie worked his mouth. He looked at the dashboard.

"Hey," said Shug. "Don't worry about it. Everything'll be fine, I told you. Relax."

Shug pressed a button on the radio. Nothing. He turned one of the dials, pressed a few more buttons. Still nothing. He slapped it with the heel of his hand. "Fuck's sake."

"It doesn't work," said Charlie.

Shug smiled. "There y'are, radio doesn't work. Better off without her. Listen, now you're talking, where d'you want dropped off?"

Charlie blinked.

"I'm serious. Where were you off to before I ruined your day?"

"Home."

"And where's that?"

"No."

"No?"

"You're not taking me home."

"What's the matter?"

"No."

"I'll drop you off right at your door, Charlie —"

"You're not coming to my home." Charlie shook his head, looked scared.

"Okay," said Shug. "Then wherever you want to be dropped off, I'll drop you off."

"Here."

"I'm not dropping you here."

"You said wherever."

"We're on a fucking motorway."

"You said —"

"You'll get yourself killed. I'm not having that on my conscience." Shug breathed out, felt the irritation rumble away. "Listen, I know you're scared and everything, but you don't have to be daft about it. I'll drop you off somewhere safe, alright?" He held up one hand before Charlie had a chance to answer. "You don't want me to take you home, that's fine. How about the town centre? You can get the bus from there, can't you?"

Charlie moved his shoulders. Let out a shaky breath.

Shug glanced at him. "I'm trying to do the right thing here."

"Then get out of my car."

"Charlie —"

Charlie's voice jumped up in volume: "Get out of my car and leave me *alone*."

Silence between them. The thrum of the car on the road.

Shug said quietly, "You know I can't do that. And do yourself a favour, Charlie — don't make the wrong thing look easy by giving us lip. I'm trying to be fair with you. You piss us off, I can't guarantee anything. I mean, I've been working on it, but it's a long road, know what I mean?"

He breathed out, shook his head. Wet his lips and realised he'd been accelerating all this time. He slowed the car, looked in the rear view. No police.

"So. Where do you want dropped?" he said.

Charlie thought about it for a long time.

Then he said, "Linlithgow."

"Linlithgow. Okay. Anywhere in particular?"

"No."

"Middle of town do you?"

Charlie nodded.

"Good. That didn't hurt now, did it?"

The look on the old man's face said otherwise. Charlie kept quiet the rest of the journey. Shug didn't try to talk to him again, knew he was a lost cause. Didn't matter what Shug did, how he tried to make it easier on him, all the old bastard saw was a youngster jacking his Micra.

That was fine. It was all his Granda would've seen, too. Only difference was, if it'd been his Granda who'd been jacked, Shug wouldn't have been driving very long. Granda would've fought tooth and nail until one of them was unconscious or dead, because Granda didn't suffer anyone gladly, especially people trying to take what was his.

There was a ticking sound somewhere deep in the engine by the time they got to the town centre. Shug pulled the Micra up in front of The Cross, which was about as central as you could get. He looked out the window, saw people on the Saturday shop, kids and parents, a small gang of young lads on bikes up the way there. He was out in the open, and it was stupid to stay much longer. He looked across at Charlie. The old man didn't move.

"Listen," he said, "they didn't give us much, but you're welcome to it." Shug pulled thirty quid's worth of fivers out of his jacket pocket. "For your trouble and everything."

Charlie looked at the money, but didn't take it. Shug leaned over and tucked the notes into the breast pocket of Charlie's blazer, patted it smooth and then straightened his poppy.

"Alright then, on you go."

Charlie didn't move. His eyes were glazed, pink in the corners. He looked as if he was close to tears. And there was nothing sadder than a grown man in tears.

"Come on now, Charlie. Chop-chop. Don't want to make us late, do you?"

Charlie turned to him. His chin wobbled.

"Please," he said.

Shug undid his seat belt and got out of the car. He surveyed the people passing by — nobody was watching him — and went round to the passenger side. He pulled open the door, saw Charlie flinch at the sight of him. He leaned over, clicked Charlie's seat belt open, let it whip back over the old man's shoulder. Then he stepped back. Waited.

"Don't make this difficult," he said.

Charlie shifted in his seat. Looked at the steering wheel.

"I'm not pissing about, Charlie. Be sensible and get out of the car."

Charlie let out a sigh and got out of the car, his shoulders hunched. Shug slammed the door as soon as he was clear, headed back round to the driver's side.

He stopped before he got in, leaned on the roof. "You feel free to phone this in any time you want, alright? Sooner the better. Don't want them to think you're pulling a fast one, do we?"

Shug ducked into the car, shut the door. He crunched gears as he pulled away, that ticking sound turning into a rattle. He glanced back at Charlie in the rear view. Rain began to spot the windscreen.

He hoped the old bloke got somewhere dry soon, else he'd catch his death, and Shug really didn't want to be held responsible for that. He hoped that Charlie did the right thing and phoned it in, too.

But most of all he hoped that rattle in the engine wasn't anything serious. It was a long way to California, after all.

2.

A couple of miles out of Linlithgow, the rattle was louder than the rain. Not long after that, the rattle turned into a persistent cough. By the time Shug hit Sandburn, the cough was tubercular. Finally, when it sounded as if the Micra needed a priest, Shug turned it to the shoulder, let the engine hack its last while he watched rain snakes on the windscreen and breathed slowly through his mouth.

Anger was a deluded mind.

Anger exaggerated something's faults.

Anger prompted an escalation to a negative emotional climax. It was unproductive, it was unnecessary, but it was also completely unavoidable.

"The question," whispered Shug, "is how do you deal with this negative emotion in a healthy and progressive way?"

Very good question, and not the first time

he'd asked it. Normally the answer was count to ten and take deep breaths, exhale the rage a little on each number until it faded away. There was nothing wrong with getting angry, but there was something wrong with not questioning *why* he was angry. Because if he didn't question his negative emotional state, then he was letting it rule his rational mind, make his decisions for him.

And that was no way to live.

So Shug focused on what made him feel angry right now, then he worked out a rational response to it.

Shug got out of the car, went to the boot. He found a length of rubber hose and an old pop bottle, which he used to siphon the petrol out of the tank. Then he doused the inside of the car and dropped a flaming Swan Vesta into the puddle. The seat caught orange, spread and smoked. Shug cracked the window a little to let the air get in, and then shut the door.

Wasn't the situation that had boiled his piss. He had to be clear about that. No, what had made him angry was his own decision to jack a pensioner's car. In hindsight, it didn't make a lot of sense. Yes, Charlie was an easy target, but pensioners ran their rides to rust, let the little problems get big because they were too tight to pay for repairs. He should've jacked someone younger driving a newer model. That way he wouldn't be out here in the pissing rain and miles from home.

Stop. Breathe.

Accept this as a lesson learned. Time to let it go and move on.

Shug walked backwards, watching the Micra's windows smoke up, then turned and tugged his collar vertical. He took to the road, preferring the tarmac to the mud of the ditch, his hands in his pockets and his head down.

It was a setback, he thought. That was all. He'd get round it. All he had to do was keep his goal in mind.

California.

When people asked him where he was from, that was what he said. The California Shug called home was four big streets and a B road, set slap bang in the pretty part of Falkirk, which wasn't saying much. The biggest thing he could remember happening to the town was Governor Arnold Schwarzenegger. Arnie wrote the people of California a letter once, something to do with International Scots Appreciation Day or something. Anyway, it was short and patronising, but people were proud of it. The way Shug saw it, the letter wasn't worth the ink. His California was the kind of place people left as soon as they could. And they never came back, not unless they absolutely had to.

Just as Shug absolutely had to. Four years on, the place was only just preferable to his Saughton cell. He wouldn't be there long, mind. An hour, maybe less, and he was gone for good. The big thing to watch was his temper, because if anything was going to fuck this up, it was that.

It was his biggest weakness. His temper, coupled with poor impulse control, had gotten him banged up. That was what the therapist told him, anyway. Shug had gone a year thinking it was bad luck, but it turned out to be his own fault.

The therapist was a long man in short trousers, showed three inches of pale, hairy skin every time he sat down. He wore thick glasses over small eyes. The first three weeks, Shug didn't pay attention to a word the bloke said. He was too busy trying to figure out who he looked like.

Week four, it came to him.

Jarvis Cocker.

"You're all here for a reason," said Jarvis. "And not because you broke the law." He adjusted his glasses and looked at the ceiling. "You're here because you have ... *feelings*. You have emotions that sometimes override your intelligence." He moved his lips. "Yes, you're intelligent. And sane. I look around here today and I can see bright, reasonable men who have one major thing in common — they act daft when they're annoyed."

There was a grim silence. Shug and the other six wanted to pound Jarvis into the fucking floor. Prick had a mouth on him, and it sounded like he was using it to take the piss.

"You see? Already thinking daft." The therapist cleared his throat, leaned forward in his chair. "And what I'm here to do is get you gentlemen talking about it. Because if you don't talk about it, you don't face it. And if you don't face it, then you can't control it. Do you see?"

They didn't. Not for a while, anyway.

By week ten, the room echoed with recrimination. Jarvis told them to talk about the things that made them angry, then dissect why that was the case. The same conclusions came back time and again: they got angry because they felt they weren't in control, wasn't that right? And most of the impulse control issues that had landed them behind bars, well, weren't they based in an urge to rebel against this lack of control, to seize it back for themselves?

Shug agreed. It was easier than arguing, which was what Jarvis wanted. He wanted you to lose your temper, provide him with another example to pick apart in front of the others.

Shug didn't play that. He swallowed it back, and soon he could pass for calm even when he was raging. It meant he didn't have to talk about Fiona or any of the rest of it, and it meant that Jarvis ticked the right boxes when it came to his licence.

It wasn't all bollocks, mind. Some of what Jarvis said to them made sense. Like the time he told them: "One of the reasons — and do correct me if I'm wrong here, gentlemen, this is a free room, after all — but one of the reasons I believe many of you may struggle with your temper is that you don't have a long-term goal."

Silence to that. The men sat and thought about it. Shug looked at the blank faces around him.

"Hugh," said Jarvis. "What do you think?"

"Think?"

"Yes."

"About what?"

"About a goal."

"I don't have one?"

"You don't have one," said Jarvis, nodding. "Which is my point exactly. You have nothing to look forward to, nothing to work for, so you have nothing to lose. You live purely in the moment."

"Yes," said Shug.

"Perhaps, gentlemen, instead of doing that, instead of living in the moment, perhaps you could make a conscious decision to live in the *future*, hmm?" Jarvis smiled at them. "Perhaps, instead of letting your brains charge ahead, you could take a breath — just one deep breath like the ones we've practised, right from the gut — and when you breathe out you could picture your goal. Yes? Your end point. Wherever *you* want to be."

Jarvis let that one sit with the group for a few seconds before he glanced at his watch and leaned back in his chair.

"Okay," he said, "I think that's about all we have time for this session. For next time, though, I want you to have a good long think about what your goal might be, okay? I want you to think of something, some kind of ambition, that might give you pause the next time your temper threatens to get the better of you. Really give it some thought, because we'll be sharing with the group, okay?"

Shug did as he was told. He thought about Fiona, but that didn't work. By that time, she didn't want anything to do with him. So for the first time in a long time he thought beyond her. He thought about his home town, and the name made him tinker with the restricted internet access in the library.

That was when he found Captain Robert Dollar. A random click, a search on Falkirk, and there he was. Dollar was a Falkirk lad, made his fortune in logging and freight, established the Falkirk Cultural Center, which were three words you didn't often see in such close proximity. He was also connected to Bohemian Grove which, if you wanted to talk about a hotbed of political intrigue and power, that was the place to be. The richest of the rich paid a lot of money to dick about in costumes up there, and Dollar was the man with the deed.

So, if you had to pick a role model, thought Shug, you could do a lot worse.

The Falkirk Cultural Center was in San Rafael, California. There was even an Inverness around there somewhere further to the west. The more Shug played with Google Maps, the more he felt that he was reaching the first strikes of an idea. He had pictures of California in his head, beaches and palm trees, Hollywood and orange juice. More than that, crystallizing now, becoming something that he never knew he wanted before. And he never knew it because it wasn't something he'd ever really thought about. It wasn't something he'd ever been expected to think about. But looking through those pictures, he realised what his goal was.

Wine.

Never drank a glass of it in his life that hadn't come from either a box or a litre bottle, but there it was, like someone tweaking a switch in the back of his head.

Sonoma, Napa, the vineyards, the sunshine, the rolling hills. It came to him in a rush, and he didn't know what to do with himself. He shook with envy at the photos of tourist wandering blithely through the wineries. For the first time in his life, he had a dream, and it made him want to laugh until he cried.

He wasn't the only one. Colin Knox laughed when Shug mentioned it in the next session. Shug wanted to pan his face in with the chair. But he didn't. There was a sunkissed future ahead of him if he played his cards right. And the more he thought about it, the more his plans began to seem concrete. So by the time his date came round and his probation officer signed him off, Shug had planned his itinerary to the second.

But now, thanks to Charlie's shitty motor, that itinerary was well out of the window.

Still, Shug refused to let it get to him, just as he refused to let the rain wear him down or the cold wind him up. He'd be fine soon enough, just had to keep walking. He nodded to himself. Rain ran down the bridge of his nose, and he sniffed it.

The sign up ahead read two miles to California.

If only it was that bloody simple.

3.

When he got to California, it was pitch black and pouring. On a wall behind the Sunshine Village sign were two lads in slick hoodies and shiny puffer jackets. One had a large bottle of blue WKD, the other a fat roll-up that sent a sweet smell into the rain and illuminated the inside of his hands every time he puffed on it. They both watched Shug as he approached, swapping the bottle with the spliff. The one with the bottle raised it to his lips with both hands, a baby in a boiler jacket, sucking on booze.

Shug's internal alarm went off. They would say something if he went past them, and no matter what that something was, the way he was feeling, it wouldn't take much to get him raging.

Another thing he'd learned — when you see a situation that's liable to make you lose your temper, take charge of it up front.

"Y'alright, son?" said Shug.

The one with the spliff hawked and spat into a puddle.

"Good weather for ducks, eh?"

No reply.

"You fellas ken Fiona Paterson?"

The spliff hoodie blew smoke. It didn't drift far before it was beaten into nothing by the rain. The lads swapped drink and smoke.

"Used to live up this way," said Shug, still watching them. "Forty-three."

"Eh?" said the drinker.

"I'm asking youse, d'you ken Fiona Paterson?"

The sound of booze sloshing back into the bottle. The hoodie with the blue moustache said, "Fuck you on?"

"So you don't know her."

"Fuck dae ah fuckin' ken yer fuckin' wumman eh?"

"Alright, then," said Shug. "Nice talking to you. Have a good night."

He turned away, braced himself for the bottle thrown at his back. Didn't happen, probably because there was still a good swallie or two left in it and these boys had to make it last. Part of him still wanting them to try something, just to see if he could sidestep the conflict when he was wet through and sick to fucking death of walking. But they weren't playing it. Which was fine. Shug was positive there'd be something else to test his resolve. He just hoped Fiona was where he left her. If she wasn't, that would put a crimp in his plans that no amount of deep breathing and visualisation would help. He needed her to be there. He needed a constant. And if she wasn't, then these lads could expect a return visit.

That wasn't healthy. Had to stop that. Had to focus on the long-term.

Shug hadn't told her he was getting out. Didn't think it was necessary at the time. Forewarned was forearmed, and he had to catch her off-guard, see her as she really was now. After all, the last time they talked, she ended it by storming off in a huff, and he didn't exactly go chasing after her. *Couldn't* go chasing after her without a couple of fucking screws putting him to the lino. He'd been six months into the stretch, the group work still in its early stages, and while he didn't remember now what they'd been fighting about, it was probably enough for him to threaten her with a smack in the mouth. Because that was the way he used to talk to her in those days. It was the way he used to talk to everyone.

He arrived at the front gate. No lights in the windows. Curtains were pulled back, too. He brushed water off his watch, pressed the glow button. Wasn't seven yet. Back in the day, she'd be home and on with the tea by now. He looked back down the road, saw the edge of the sign, the glow of a mobile phone and thought he heard laughter.

He pushed open the gate. It bounced off the fence. He leaned on the doorbell.

Waited.

Nothing.

Tried it again. And then again. The fourth time was shorter, an urge to lean on it until it stuck caught and discarded.

She wasn't in. Not a problem. Didn't know where she was, but that didn't matter.

He looked up, caught a face full of rain. Then he blinked the water away and headed for the side of the house, followed the path round. He stumbled over what looked like off-cuts of wood, kicked them idly with one foot before he continued to the back of the house. There he looked up at the windows again. Still no light.

He remembered a different back door round here. Wooden, rickety, easy to kick down. Instead there were two brand new UPVC French doors. Shug put two hands up on the glass, looked inside. If he didn't know better, he would've sworn this was someone else's place. The ratty old lino had gone from the kitchen floor, replaced by a light-coloured laminate.

Shug stepped back and chewed on his bottom lip. He weighed up his options quickly and calmly. He was extensive, rational. Then he went back round to the side of the house, picked up a length of wood and put it through the glass in one of the French doors. An almighty crash that the whole street must've heard, but Shug didn't care. He put his hand through, felt around for the key that he knew would be sticking out the lock.

He stepped into the kitchen and closed the door behind him. Moved away from the shrill, wet breeze that came in through the hole. He dripped onto the laminate, part of him still convinced that he'd broken into the wrong house. Then he saw the photo of Fi on the fridge. He plucked it out from under the cheeseburger magnet, held it up to the light. She was smiling. Her hair was a lighter colour, sun-bleached. She was with an ugly woman, big nose and squinty eyes, probably one of her mates down the kindergarten. He tapped the photo, then slapped it back onto the fridge door.

He squelched through to the front room and turned on the light. It was laminate in here, too. New chrome-looking fire in the fireplace. New telly, flat and black, in the corner. Modern, hard-edged sofa. Not Fiona's taste. Not the taste she used to have, anyway. Everything looked wipe-clean. He noticed some brightly coloured plastic toys in the corner of the room, looked like they'd belong to a dog. He went over, picked up a blue and red rubber microphone. He shook it; it rattled. He blinked at it.

Didn't know what to think. His brain had frozen. He stood staring at the dog toy for a good minute until the hum of the fridge snapped him out of it.

No distractions. Couldn't waste time standing here like a twat when there was work to do.

Shug tossed the microphone onto the sofa and made for the stairs. He took them two at a time and when he hit the landing, he went straight for the main bedroom. He opened the door to his own reflection, drowned rat, staring at him from mirrored wardrobes that ran the length of one wall. Shug turned on a bedside lamp as he walked round to the right hand side of the bed — *his* side of the bed — then he got down on his knees, started tugging at the corner of the carpet.

It wouldn't budge.

Tugged at it again, but there wasn't much give. He kept at it until he felt fabric rip under his aching fingers. Once he pulled up the corner, he tore it right across.

Underneath, he saw the large gap between

the floorboards, the crack in one of them that meant Shug hadn't lost his fucking mind. He prised up the board, stuck one hand into the hole.

He felt around far longer than he needed to, then brought his hand up empty bar dust and fluff. He sat back against the side of the bed and stared at the wall.

Okay. Fine.

It was gone.

Course it was.

Downstairs, the sound of a key in the front door. He got to his feet, killed the bedside lamp, and listened.

The door closed. There was a voice, female. Could've been Fiona, but Shug wasn't sure. She was struggling with something.

Shug moved to the bedroom door.

Another voice. At least, he thought it was. Either a voice, or a small animal making a noise. Might've been a dog. That would explain the toys. He watched the light click on in the hall downstairs. Some movement, some more animal noises. Something plastic knocked against the wall. Another light went on, probably the kitchen.

When he heard her swear — "Oh, *fuck's* sake" — he knew it was Fiona.

Shug went downstairs as coolly as he could.

She heard him, and rattled through the cutlery drawer. When he hit the ground floor and turned to the kitchen, he saw her braced and ready to attack, a large triangular knife in both hands.

She didn't, mind. Didn't attack, didn't do much of anything. Just stood there staring at him.

"Hullo, Fi," he said.

She shuffled her feet. Breathed through her mouth. He thought for a second she didn't recognise him, or maybe she did and thought he'd gone prison soft. It happened. He waited for her. No hurry.

"Shug," she said.

"That's right."

"Shuggie, *Jesus*."

"How are you?"

"I'm ..." She lowered the knife, swallowed. "You're ..."

"I'm home."

"You're out."

"That's right."

"What d'you want?"

"What d'you think?"

She blinked. "I don't know."

Shug smiled. "Where is it, Fiona?"

"Where's what?"

He looked at the knife. The tip shook. "You

know what."

Fiona opened her mouth to say something, but there was that small animal noise again. A whimpering sound, somewhere behind him in the front room. It was followed by a rattle.

"You get a dog?" he said.

"What?"

He moved back down the hall, stuck his head round the door.

A toddler sat strapped into a pushchair. He had the microphone in one hand and was busy shaking it. He stopped when he saw Shug, raised the toy to his mouth and chewed on it. His face was open, his eyes wide. He removed the microphone and rattled it at Shug before it fell out of his hand onto the floor.

Shug looked back at Fiona. Her face was grey in the light from the strip directly above her. The knife hung loosely from one hand.

He swallowed against a rush of anger, counted slowly to ten.

Fiona said, "Shug, I meant to —"

"Put the kettle on," he said, digging around in his pocket for his Lamberts. "We've got some catching up to do."

4.

Shug blew smoke and said, "I'll tell you, Fi, I'm a changed man. Well, mostly. It's not that easy, like, when stuff keeps happening, y'know?"

"You want another tea?"

"Nah, it's fine. It's okay." He picked up his third mug of tea in an hour and drained it. Thoughts of the chippy up the road made his gut gurgle, but this had to be dealt with first.

"Won't take a second."

"Sit down," he said.

Fiona sat down slowly.

Sad to say, but it was better to let Fiona think that he was still the kind of man who could kick back his chair and plant a hard right on her if she gave him lip. Better to play like it was back in the day, back when he was a bastard. Sad he had to do that, but sometimes people didn't believe in the capacity for change. They saw what they wanted to see. And what Fiona saw right now was a man who'd reddened her cheek more than once. If he thought about it for long enough, he'd feel guilty.

No. Acceptance *without* guilt.

It was fine. That was the past. He'd forgiven himself for it. Now was different. Now was acting. He smiled at the end of his cigarette.

"How was it?" she said.

"Okay once I got settled in, like. Got to know the place a bit. Not as much as some people would've liked, mind, but well enough."

"You're out early."

"Not really."

"I thought it was seven years they gave you."

"It was. But if you keep your nose clean —"

"Oh aye?" she said.

"Aye." Shug tapped ash from the Lambert into the saucer beside him, its bottom already laced with ash and one screwed up filter. He'd offered Fi, but she didn't smoke. Bad for the bairn. Shug didn't give a fuck. He breathed out. "Don't blame you thinking I'd do every one of 'em. Things change, though, eh?"

"Do they?"

"Changed here."

Fiona raised her eyebrows.

"Done up nice," said Shug. "New floors, new telly. Must've set you back."

"It's been a while."

"Telling us you saved up."

She sipped her tea. If it was anything like Shug's it'd gone cold about ten minutes back, but Fiona pretended like it was still hot, both hands around the mug, held high in front of her face. He wanted to knock it out of her grip, but he stayed still.

"Yeah?" he said.

She nodded.

"Don't blame you. A bairn running around, working all the hours, you got to treat yourself every now and then." He sniffed. "Life's hard enough. You need some creature comforts, something to look forward to, something to come home to. You know that's what they told us inside? You've got to have something to come home to. Something to live for." He pointed into some intangible future. "Long-term."

He stared at her. She stared at the table.

"So," he said. "You know I checked."

She nodded.

"So it's not there."

Another nod.

"Going to tell us where it is?"

Fiona rubbed at her cheek, showed teeth. "Not here."

"Listen, if you spent the money, I'm not going to get angry. Some people out there probably reckon you deserve it for putting up with us all those years, maybes even see it as my way of providing for you while I was away —"

"I didn't take your money."

He tapped the side of his mug. It didn't make much of a sound. "Then where is it?"

There was some snuffling in the front room, turned into a whimper. The bairn crying for his mother. Shug heard the first stuttered breaths of a crying jag. Course she hadn't taken any money. She didn't need it. She had a job, and the bairn's father would be chipping in, most likely. He watched her for a few seconds, trying to connect the women in front of him with the one who stormed out of a visiting room three and a half years back. That woman was a girl, spoiled and lippy. This one seemed different, harder. It was probably the bairn. Kids changed people.

The bairn started crying. Fiona stood.

"Where you going?" he said.

"See the bairn," she said, and didn't wait for permission.

He twisted round in his chair, watched her leave. He smoked his cigarette down to the filter, then ground it out. Reached for another one, but it was too wet to light. He left it broken in the saucer and smacked his lips. His mouth was dry. Should've had that extra cup.

The crying stopped. Shug got out of his seat and went through to the front room. She stood with the toddler in the crook of her arm, a mobile in her free hand. Shug leaned against the doorway. He watched her push a couple of buttons with her thumb before he said, "Didn't hear it ring."

She looked up, then back at the phone as if it was poisonous. She hefted the kid. "Missed call."

"Who?"

"Didn't leave a message."

Shug held out one hand. "Give."

She hesitated, but held out the phone to him. Shug glanced at the mobile, put it in his pocket. Hadn't the foggiest about how to work it, and he wasn't going to learn with an audience. "Listen, I know you weren't expecting us back so soon, Fi. And I know you've been busy while I was away. But if you think I'm going to fuck you over because you did the same to me, you've got it wrong. Like I said, I'm a changed man. I'm not the same bloke who went in. Now I don't expect you to believe that, or understand it, or anything like that. If I'm honest, I don't really give a fuck either way. So I think I'm being reasonable with you. Not raised my voice. Not threatened you. Just asking you one question, and you're not answering it."

"Your stash," she said.

"Aye."

"It's not here."

"I know that."

"I gave it to Ailsa."

"Why'd you do that?"

"I didn't want it in the house."

"Nothing dangerous in there." He looked at the kid. "Nothing going to hurt wee whatshisname here."

"No," she said. "I know that. But it was yours. And I didn't want anything of yours in this house. You know why."

Shug spiked his initial reaction, looked around the room. She'd done everything she could to clear his presence out of her life. Made sense, but it didn't stop that flare in his chest. Didn't stop him showing it, either. Fiona hugged the kid, regarded him defiantly. Like if he started swinging, she was willing to go all the way. She'd turned that petulance to strength. Shug wondered when that had happened.

Again, probably the kid.

"Okay," he said. He pushed off the doorway, went back through to the kitchen to retrieve his Lamberts. She didn't want his shit in the house, she didn't want him in the house, he didn't want to be in the house, there was a simple solution.

It was better this way, anyway. He'd meant to pop in on Ailsa, say goodbye. This made it easier.

There was a knock at the front door. Shug turned to see Fiona coming out of the front room. He saw two figures behind the frosted glass, thought for a second they were police until he remembered Fiona's mobile. He checked for the last number called.

Another mobile, called yesterday. He pressed more buttons, frowned.

No missed call.

Another knock. Shug stepped slightly back into the kitchen, hidden from the hall, but still open enough so that he could see. An old hiding place, and one he was glad was still available. He glanced back at the kitchen table, saw the large knife Fiona'd had for defence.

Fiona opened the front door.

There were two men there, and it took Shug a moment to recognise them. Another moment after that to realise that he probably wouldn't need the knife.

Len Mullan. Behind him, Golly McDonald. Life had been either extremely good to these lads, or extremely bad. They'd done some drinking since Shug saw them last, their faces beetroot with the spirits and their guts thick. Golly in particular had the butter churn beginnings of a serious weight problem. They were both smiling, but neither looked comfortable.

"He here?" said Len.

"If he is me, then aye," said Shug.

"Shuggie fuckin' Boyle," said Len. His teeth were so small, he had to open his mouth to grin.

"Uh-huh."

"Long fuckin' time."

"Not that long, though, eh? How'd you know?"

"Fiona."

"Oh aye?" Shug looked at Fiona. She was busy in the front room with the kid. Shug looked back at Len, tried to see if there was any resemblance.

"Texted us," said Len.

"I see."

"I ken that look. It's nothing bad. Honest, man, you've got to chill out."

"Aye, maybes. Listen, it's good to see you lads, but I've got to be getting on."

"Why's that, you're no' staying?"

"No."

Golly's face crumpled. "What, were you just going to leave?"

"No offence, Golly, but I've got to be elsewhere."

"And where's that?" said Len.

"Elsewhere."

"It's near Falkirk," said Golly.

"I know it," said Len. "Not that fuckin' far, is it? C'mon and have a few drinks, Shug."

Shug shook his head.

"Ach, you will." Len put a heavy hand on Shug's shoulder as Golly opened the door for them. "Dinnae be fuckin' daft, Shugs, eh? Me and you and Golly, we go back too far for you to just up and fuckin' leave us without a send-off. Got a lot to catch up on, don't we, Gol?"

"Oh, aye," said Golly.

So Ailsa would have to wait, because these two had the smell of unfinished business on them. Shug found himself nodding, ushered out of the house by Len. And when he glanced back at Fiona, she was crying.

5.

Four years, three months, six days ago.

A post office in Bathgate, one big cluttered front window, a cash machine set into the wall. Outside, there was an advert for Walls ice creams and a stolen Punto with the engine running. Inside the Punto were Shug, Len and Golly. Golly sat in the driver's seat, tapping along to the slow beat of the Sam and Dave song on the radio. Len was in the back seat. Shug watched him sweat in the rear view mirror, then turned back to the post office. "Just remember your mark and you'll be fine, alright?"

"Aye," said Len.

"Follow my lead."

"I fuckin' ken, alright?"

"Alright."

Shug got out of the Punto, slammed the door behind him. He walked across the road to the post office, the weight under his jacket knock-ing against his ribs. He patted the pocket with the ski mask in it, just to make sure it was still there, then pushed into the post office.

Sweets and cigarettes on his left, magazines and newspapers on his right. At the back, a long, windowed post office counter, about three or four foot deep.

An Asian couple ran the place. He was small, thin and bald, wore milk bottle glasses. She was round and hidden under vast swathes of mate-rial. Her eyes were sunk so dark she looked as if she was wearing glasses too. Or at least looked as if she needed them, the way she peered at Shug as he entered. He went to the till, bought a pack of Lamberts and a Lion bar. When her back was turned, he glanced across at the post office part. The man worked behind the glass, counting something and talking quietly to his customer. He smiled, but then he had one of those faces that always looked as if it was smiling, his teeth too big for his mouth.

Shug paid for the cigarettes and chocolate. He turned from the woman, wandered over to the magazine rack as he waited for the customer to finish off. He moved down the rack, looking without touching at the fishing, motoring, hand-icraft magazines. When the customer at the post office was done and moving towards the exit, Shug looked out the front window to see Len getting out of the Punto.

Lad had timing.

When Len shut the door, Golly flinched.

Shug felt for the ski mask in his pocket, brought it out as the bell above the front door rang and Len entered. There was a school of thought that said there was no point going in there and then pulling on the mask, but that school of thought reckoned on people remembering anything other than the gun pointed right at them. Shug pulled the wool over his face and turned back to the woman. Len made a beeline for the post office, his mask already on.

The woman saw Len, let out a screech. Shug showed her the double-barrel. She saw nothing but a fallen eight and the screech cut short.

Len had his pistol drawn and pointed at the man behind the counter. He barked orders, told him to open the fucking door else he'd put all six through the fucking glass. Shug knew he wouldn't. Fact of the matter was, both the shotgun and the pistol were empty. It was the difference between a short hitch and a life sentence if it all went pear-shaped. And Shug didn't trust himself not to unload into the first cunt that gave him grief. Didn't trust a high-strung lad like Len to keep his head, either. Too much of the cowboy about him.

The bloke behind the counter started shouting back, freaking like a trapped squirrel, made himself a moving target. Swearing at Len. Calling him names in two different languages. Shug shouted once at the man, then struck the woman hard across the bridge of the nose with the short butt of the sawn-off. She buckled and dropped. She grabbed sweets on the way, brought Twirls and Kit Kats down on top of her. Shug shifted round the counter in time to see her eyes flicker closed.

Silence from the bloke. Shug could hear Len breathing hard behind his mask. He had the barrel of the pistol pressed against the glass.

"Open the door," said Len.

Shug aimed the sawn-off at the wife. Looked up at the bloke behind the counter, thickened his accent when he said, "Dinnae be fuckin' daft and open that fuckin' door else I'll fuckin' dae the cunt."

The bloke opened the door.

Len moved quickly, shoved him up against the wall. "Knuckle the fuckin' wall, son, and don't you fuckin' move, alright?"

The man put his hands up, Len pushed his back and knuckles to the wall. He looked pinned in place. Len shook out a bin bag and went for the drawers. Cleared them of cash, took some stamps, postal orders, whatever he could lay fingers on.

There should have been alarms. There were alarms in Shug's head, but the only real noise was the rustle of the bin bags and his own rasping breath.

He blinked.

And there was Len, out from behind the post office counter, one black bag full to bursting, the pistol still pointed at the bloke. Shug stepped over the woman on the floor and emptied the till. Then he and Len clattered out the front door.

It was drizzling. Hard to see. Shug tore the mask from his head, stuffed it into his jacket pocket. Len launched himself into the back of the Punto, rolled the bag across the floor. Shug hit the passenger seat just as Golly floored it and the car doors shut themselves. That was the thing about Golly — he was too gangly, too recognisable, the albino bastard, his hair out like blond springs — but he was quick enough behind the wheel, and he was good at gutting the motors when they were finished.

He was good at getting them out of there, too.

Five seconds, then ten, and they were on the A road.

"Ya fucker," said Shug.

"Ya fucker's right." Len grinned through his

mask, pawing the money out of the bin bag.

"Take your mask off, man. Have the fuckin' polis on us."

Len tugged at the mask, chucked it onto the seat next to him, but didn't take his eyes off the cash. "How much did you say was going to be there, Shugs?"

"Ten, fifteen on giro day. Bit more in the till."

Len laughed. Shug turned a little in his seat. "Why, what you got?"

"I don't know, but it's more than fifteen."

Golly looked in the rear view. Shug nudged him, told him to keep his eyes on the road.

Turned out Len was right. It was more than fifteen. Twenty-three grand in total, split three ways with the surplus tossed for, which left each with about eight grand, give or take. Len wanted to get the bottles in, Shug told him to hang fire for at least a week. No sense in drawing attention to themselves. Didn't want to extend an open invitation to the law, did they?

Of course they didn't. So Shug stashed his cut with his passport and his Granda's watch in a shoebox, put that shoebox under the floorboards in the bedroom and went on with his life. Told Fiona where it was just in case something happened to him. In hindsight, he reckoned he must've known something was going to happen.

In hindsight, mind, everything looked pre-ordained. That was the killer.

The police were round Fiona's house the next day. Two bull uniforms and two CID, asking him all sorts of questions about where he'd been, what he'd been doing, did he know Leonard Mullan and Derek McDonald. Shug gave them vague answers and tried his best to figure out what the fuck had tipped them, or who. Because even when it got to court, Shug didn't see the moment that had tipped the police to him in particular. There were eye witnesses, right enough — turned out the woman had remembered a lot more than the sawn-off — and the Punto hadn't been burned as well as Golly normally did, but that didn't explain why he was the only one pulled, and why he was the only one sent down.

And the only thing that could explain that were the two men on either side of him now. Golly taking long strides, chattering away to himself and nobody else, Len with one hand squarely in the middle of Shug's back, breathing lager into the night air and smiling.

"You've got some timing, eh?" said Len. "There's me and Gol going to go down the pub –"

"Don't let me stop you."

"Nah, it's crowded with cunts."

"Pricks to a man," said Golly.

"We'll do better with what we've got in the house, what d'you think?"

"Oh, aye."

"Got the *good* stuff in, Shugs," said Len and slapped him between the shoulder blades. "Almost like we knew you was coming."

"Almost," said Shug.

As they approached Len's house, Len tossed Golly the keys to his front door. Golly ran ahead to open up.

"It's good to have you back," said Len. "Seriously."

"Can't stay for long, Len."

"Ach, never mind about that. We'll give you a braw send-off, eh?"

Shug nodded, but didn't say anything else as he was escorted to the front door and then into the house, where it smelled of cheap resin and takeaways.

All this time, and some things never changed. It was almost comforting.

Almost.

6.

Whisky and beer, the whisky nicked, the beer out of code. Both cheap and nasty, the kind of booze people drank when they all they cared about was getting off their face. Shug had tried to remember Captain Dollar's rules, chief of which was don't get pissed, but if he didn't drink, he wouldn't leave. He nursed his can. He tipped the whisky to his lips, already cracked and burning, and he watched Len and Golly knock back the booze like someone was going to take it off them.

That wasn't new. The boys had always liked a drink. They were only human.

But it wasn't just the booze now, was it? There was something else going on, something that had bought the new telly, the array of consoles under it, the DVDs and Blu-Rays scattered on the lino by the games. This was something that meant quick money, and because Len was stunted, he'd spent it just as quickly. In the background, a mini hi-fi played west coast rap. Same shite he'd listened to when he was a kid.

"So what you been doing with yourselves all this time?" said Shug.

"Business," said Len.

"Ah, right y'are. *Business*."

Len was leaning back in a gaming chair, rocking slightly with a half pint of whisky held in both hands. Staring at Shug like he was ready for anything. "Once you got took, Shugs, we had to have a word with ourselves, ken what I mean?"

"I see."

"Robberies weren't the way to go, were they, Gol?"

Golly shook his head, obscured by a cloud of weed smoke. He made a series of little coughing noises, then added to the cloud by exhaling. "Too much risk."

"No risk for you," said Shug.

"Ah now —"

"You were the driver. You weren't in there."

"Hey, still risky, Shug." Golly sniffed. "Something happens to youse two, I'm a sitting duck, aren't I?"

"Exactly," said Len.

"So," said Shug.

"So we decided to pool our resources, didn't we?"

"Aye."

"And do what?" said Shug, even though he knew the answer. He gestured to the telly. "You a fence now?"

Len laughed. "Do I look like a fuckin' fence?"

"Well, you don't look much like a fuckin' dealer, if that's what you're building up to."

The laugh disappeared into a cleared throat. Golly blew more smoke.

"I am, though." A quick spasm of irritation as Len caught the whine in his own voice, then: "I am a fuckin' dealer. Biggest one in the surrounding."

"Tack."

"Naw, not just. Tack. Coke. Dope. Crack."

"Give the dog a bone," said Shug.

Golly giggled. He waved a hand through the smoke, reached for his Belgian lager. Hummed to himself.

"Take the piss if you want," said Len. "We've got it fuckin' made here."

"Oh aye, it looks it. Fuckin' Scarface, this, eh? Living the high life."

"Too right," said Golly. He finished his lager and tossed the can. Pulled another from the plastic. "Got it made, Shugs. You want in —"

"There's money," said Len.

"Aye, I bet there is."

"Fuckin' serious, man. Constant. Don't have to go out to get it, neither. It comes in here."

"You deal from here."

"Aye."

"Course you do." Shug raised the can. "Then here's to your continued success, eh?"

"Fuck's that supposed to mean?" said Len.

Shug shook his head. "Nothing."

Len had stopped rocking now. He leaned forward on the chair. He sipped his whisky and swallowed.

"Honestly," said Shug. "I wish you nothing but the best."

"You can come in on it with us if you want," said Len.

Shug looked at Len, then at Golly, already mashed, and tried not to let the disgust show too much. He could come in on it with them, what a fucking treat, what an opportunity. Get stoned off his face every fucking night, slumped in front of the widescreen, watching porn and MMA until he went blind or stupid enough to get robbed by a couple of fucking kids. Because they way this was set up, that was definitely on the cards for these two. Daft thing was, they didn't even see it.

Shug lowered his eyes, pretended to think it over. Then he said, "I don't know, lads."

"What's not to know?" said Len.

"Things are a bit fucked up with us at the moment. Got some loose ends I need to tie up before I commit to a new career, know what I mean?"

"Like what?"

"Like ... What's your long-term goal, Leonard?"

"Come again?"

"Your long-term goal. Your dream."

"Make as much fuckin' money as possible," said Golly, leaning across with the spliff.

Len waved it away. "That's good enough for me an' all. Why, what's yours?"

"I want to see the world," said Shug.

"Fuck off."

"Seriously."

"When'd this happen?"

"Saughton."

"Fuck off."

"Not kidding. Had a lot of time to sit and think in there. When you get that, you get a chance to look at your priorities, and one of mine turned out that I wanted to travel a bit, see outside of the lowlands. Which is why I'm not staying long."

"You're going on holiday, then," said Golly.

"Could say that."

"What about your licence?" said Len. "You have to report in."

"I'll work something out."

Len didn't say anything. He drank his whisky. Topped up the glass. Held the bottle out to Shug, who took a couple of glugs and kept the bottle down by the side of his chair. He drank some this time, felt the violent burn at the back of his throat, felt his gut contract. He didn't show it.

Golly held out the spliff again. "Anyone want to get on that, they're more than fuckin' welcome."

"Watch yourself," said Len.

Shug looked across at Golly. His skin had gone from its usual white to green. A toke or two from whitey, and he knew it. Golly moved on the settee. Something metal showed between the cushions and the back. Shug didn't get a chance to see it in any detail before Golly moved in front of it with his beer.

"Where you going?" said Len.

"Away," said Shug.

"How long?"

"I don't know yet. Depends on if I like it there."

"Being awful secretive, Shug."

"No, I'm not."

"Like you've got something to hide."

"No."

Len smiled, but there was no humour in it.

He leaned back in his chair again. "Y'know, it's funny, when Fi texted us, I thought she was having a laugh. I said that to Gol, didn't I, Gol?"

Golly didn't say anything. Had a Stan Laurel face on him as he nodded.

"I'd be lying if I said we were expecting you out so soon, Shug."

"Same here."

"So how'd that happen, then?"

"Good behaviour."

"Fuck off."

"It's true."

"You're not the good behaviour type."

"I am now."

"Fuck off," said Len, with less conviction this time. "Mad dog like you disnae just do his fuckin' time. You're telling me there weren't incidents?"

"There's always incidents."

"What'd I tell you?"

"It's how you handle them that counts."

"And you managed to keep your fuckin' temper the whole time?" said Len, his eyes slits. "You. Of all the fuckin' people in this world to get his early licence."

"Yes."

"No."

"That's the way it happened."

"You know what I think?"

"What's that?"

"I think you kept your head down. I think you buckled under."

"You what?"

"You ken what I mean."

Golly laughed, short and sudden.

"You're asking did I turn," said Shug.

Len didn't answer. He just kept smiling. Shug wanted to plunge his fist into that grin, turn the fucker inside out.

"No," said Shug. "I didn't turn. Not like that. And if you're asking did I sell you and the boy here —"

"Who the fuck you calling a boy?" said Golly, too mashed to get too emotional. What would have been anger registering as mild irritation thanks to the tack. "Watch your fuckin' tongue, Shugs."

"If you're asking did I tell the authorities who was that masked man with me? Who was the daft twat who couldn't burn a fuckin' car properly? Then no, I didn't. Because why would I, Len? No point in telling them what they already know. What I'm more interested in is how I managed to do four in Saughton while youse two are playing New Jack City out here."

Len smiled, some of it reaching his eyes.

"Come on, now," he said.

"Fuck off, now."

"Let's have another drink, eh?"

"You brought us here to drink, aye. And I've done that. Now you do me the courtesy of answering my fuckin' question, son."

Len glanced at Golly. Golly nodded slowly and emphatically. Irritation flashed on Len's face. "Tell you what, how about we stop the fucking about, eh? Get the good stuff out." He stood, kicked the settee. "Golly, wake up, you dozy cunt. I'm going to get the good stuff."

Golly pulled himself up to a sitting position. Shug caught the metal again. He drank his beer, felt a bubble of gas burst into a belch.

"I'll away and get some glasses and then we'll be having you," said Len.

Shug watched Len leave the room. Golly had started giggling. A snort every now and then, stifled by one fist. In the background, Tupac sang about California, and the song made Shug feel a little sad that it had come to this.

"You think this is funny," said Shug, quietly.

"Naw, Shugs, naw."

"Aye, you do. Sitting there, you're playing gangster. You're loving it. The pair of you. So what's he off to get there, Gol?"

"The good stuff."

Shug picked up the bottle of whisky by the side of his chair, held it up to Golly. "The good stuff, eh? Hope so, because this is shite, this.

Wouldn't give this to the fuckin' homeless."

"You ken how it is, Shugs."

"I know how it is, Golly." Shug stood, glanced at the closed door, then over at Len's gaming chair.

Golly shifted on the settee. One hand moved towards the dip in the back of the cushions.

Shug wanted to tell Golly not to do it. He wanted to say that he knew exactly what he was doing, that there was a sawn-off down the settee there and Golly was going for it. That Golly was too fucking mashed or too fucking stupid not to realise Shug was onto him. And he just wanted to tell Golly to leave it. It didn't matter. Whatever Len had told him to do, it didn't matter. Because Shuggie Boyle was a changed man. He hadn't lied about that. He wasn't the same bloke who'd stood in the dock and said nothing. That bloke would've taken a quick and nasty revenge on whoever he thought had put him there. That bloke wouldn't have even needed the confirmation that it was either of them that'd shopped him. Chances are, he would've taken that revenge regardless, as a means of exercising his frustration at having the last four years of his life taken off him.

But he'd changed.

He was calm now. Gentle.

Which was why he turned away when he

brought the whisky bottle down across the back of Golly's head.

7.

The first blow caught Golly hard, but the bottle stayed intact. Golly jerked forward, looked like he was struck with a stomach cramp. Both hands went from the settee to the back of his head. His mouth hung open, a scream lodged behind his tonsils.

Shug shattered the bottle the second time, sent cheap whisky across the settee and lino, blood from a burst scalp quick to follow. Golly found his voice, scrambled off the settee. His legs went out from under him and he hit the floor. He grabbed at the telly to try and steady himself. Left a bloody smear on the screen, more blood spilling across his cheeks. Shug chucked the bottle neck at Len's chair and leant over, pulled the sawn-off from down the back of the settee.

Cracked the spout. Two in there. Paranoid fucking bastards.

Correct fucking bastards, as it turned out.

Whether it was there in case of chancer stick-up men, or because they were expecting him round, it didn't matter. Fact was, Golly was supposed to use this on him, at the very least to keep him in place. And for that, Shug flared enough to kick him in the ribs. Then he nipped to the side of the living room as he heard Len approach. He sucked in a deep breath.

Len burst into the room. "The fuck? Gol —"

Butt of the sawn-off, short jab to the temple, another knocked Len's nose out of whack, killed his vision with tears and got the blood flowing. Shug moved forward, put one foot over Len's, pushed both barrels against the man's knee and pulled the trigger.

A colossal explosion. Made him flinch away from the light, the heat, and the warm spray on his face. He stepped back, arm aching with the recoil. He blinked, rubbed the stinging smell of smoke from his nose. He looked across at Len, the man's leg pulverised into a sodden bloody mess, his face white, eyes as wide as his mouth. And then, over the ringing in his ears, he began to hear the screams.

"Daft lads. Had a chance to be a fuckin' man about it, you had to act like little boys."

Len flailed on the floor, trying to reach for something at his back. Shug moved quickly, shoved him onto his stomach, and tugged the drilled air pistol from the back of his jeans.

"Should've had it out, you might've had a chance to get one off. You'll remember for next time, eh?"

Len made a noise that sounded like he was drowning. Shug pushed him back upright. Len's head lolled back. About to pass out, but keeping himself awake through sheer fucking rage. "I'm gonna ... I'm gonna ..."

"What?" said Shug, breathing heavily, flexing his fingers around the trigger guard of the sawn-off. "Come on, Len-son. Say what you need to say."

"Gonna fuckin' *kill* ..."

"Me? No, you're not, Len. You're not killing nothing." Golly moved behind him. Shug backed up a step, glanced over at him. "How're you, Gol?"

Golly groaned.

"That's what I thought. See now lads, you both need to have a think about how this evening could have gone. Have a wee mull on the alternatives. Open your minds to the possibility that if you'd treated us with a wee bit more respect, not treated us like a bit player in a fuckin' gangster film, then you wouldn't be lying here with your scalp in ribbons, and you'd still have your fuckin' knee."

Len sounded as if he was trying to say "fluff" over and over again. He was fading, dropping in and out of unconsciousness.

"You keep at it, son. Don't think I don't know who grassed us up, eh? Something else to think on: I wasn't going to come round here tonight. I wasn't going to do nothing to you. I was going to leave you alone, let bygones be fuckin' bygones. But you were the one pushed it. You were the one brought us round. So all this? You did it to yourself. You know what kind of man I was, you know you got off fuckin' lucky here tonight. I could've done the pair of youse and been offski before the polis caught wind. Because, let's face it, that was what you were going to do to me, eh?"

Len grinned at Shug.

"It's why she texted you. Tell you I was there. So you'd be fuckin' ready to finish it off."

Len nodded.

Shug nodded back at him, pulled Fiona's mobile from his pocket. He went through the texts sent, found the last one.

Smiled at first, but felt it drop almost immediately.

It read: SHUG HERE DONT HURT HIM PLS

Shug read it a couple of times, dropped pauses in where he thought they should go, then cleared out of it. He turned the phone off, held it tight in one white fist. He stared at Len, who stared right back, even though his eyes were glazed and his anger draining out of him as the blood began to adhere him to the lino. Shug looked over at Golly, alive and conscious, but only just. He dropped the mobile onto the settee, nudged Golly with the side of his foot.

"Call for an ambulance before he bleeds out," said Shug. "I'd take your cuts for grassing us up, but you've got nothing worth taking."

He put the sawn-off on Len's gaming chair, turned and headed for the hall. He heard the moans, the dizzy scramble as one of them launched themselves at the weapon. Just before he slammed the front door, he heard a cry of triumph, a grunt of exertion. And just as soon as he'd cleared the door, there was an explosion behind him and council blue wood chips sprayed the path.

Shug looked back, saw Golly's familiar silhouette at the end of the hall.

He gave it a shot, at least. Shug couldn't fault him for that.

He started walking. Something stung his leg. He looked down, saw the tiny hole in his jeans, felt the trickle of blood at the top of his calf. He carried on.

Heard Jarvis's voice in his head: "Think about

it this way, Hugh, someone keeps giving you a hard time, what do you do?"

"I have a word with them."

"And if that doesn't take?"

"I have another word."

Shug heard the harsh sound of prison laughter. It echoed.

"And when *that* doesn't take," said Jarvis. "What do you do then?"

"I kill them."

The laughter cut short. The thrum of striplighting, but otherwise silent.

Jarvis said: "Then that's what you'll do to yourself if you keep allowing your temper to get the better of you."

Shug shook his head.

"You have to let your anger dissipate naturally. Healthily. Think of anger as a mixture of both emotional and physical changes. The emotional is obvious, but the physical is what I imagine pushes you towards violence, Hugh, yes? The physical change is a massive surge of energy, and that energy, well, it has to go somewhere, doesn't it? And the first instinct isn't to channel it, is it? It's to explode."

Jarvis made the childish noise of a bomb blowing up.

"You just need to breathe it out," he said.

"I just need to breathe it out," said Shug.

But he couldn't, could he? Because Shug was Shug, and he'd always be that way. Shug's Granda was called Shug, too. It was his Granda he'd been named after, his Granda everyone said he resembled. And it was his Granda who originated the family temper. Famous for it. Hard man. Miner. Worked the pits his entire life, or as good as, breathed coal dust like it was oxygen. He lost good mates in blasts, lost a few more to themselves. Like them, Granda drank his blood thin and shed everyone else's once he'd had a few, and there was nothing better than a square go to put a cap on a night out, preferably with someone who gave as good as they got. By the time little Shug showed up on the scene, Granda's face looked like a brown paper bag full of walnuts, and moved like it too.

He was a good man, mind. A good man with a terrible affliction, and Shug loved him. Course, he never said it. It wasn't something you said. Just like he never cried at the man's funeral.

Granda went the Peckinpah way, swinging his fists from the floor. Beaten into a coma in a Govan boozer when he picked a bone with five rough-hewn cunts who didn't think twice about kicking shite out of an eighty-year-old man. He slept for four days after that, hooked up to breathing and bleeping machines, before he fought them too and ended up croaking at tea time, just as one of the nurses was sitting down to watch *The Fresh Prince of Bel Air*.

Always the inconsiderate bastard.

Shug slowed as he rounded the corner into the street where Ailsa lived. He checked that nobody was following him, then sat on a low front wall.

Getting tired. He rubbed at the small wound on his leg. It didn't have the pulsing ache that came with shot, so he guessed he'd been nicked by one of the wood chips. He ran one hand over his face, closed his eyes until he felt his heart slow down.

Like Jarvis said to him, a man couldn't stay belligerent his whole life. Quite apart from the fact it would probably end in him getting kicked into a twitching paste, the rage put a strain on the heart and digestive system. It gave him warnings. It had a word with him. And if that word didn't take, it would kill him.

Shug felt himself shake. He closed his eyes. Breathed through his nose. Counted to ten, then twenty. When he hit thirty, he opened his eyes again. Black spots jumped in his vision. He looked down the road at Ailsa's house.

It would be alright. A slight lapse, that's all it was.

It would be alright once he got his stash. Then he'd be out of here.

8.

"Ailsa, open the door. It's me."

It was late, getting on for later, but they were in. Steve's Land Rover was parked out front. If the car was home, then so was he. Steve was the kind of bloke who never strayed too far from his beloved Land Rover, and if he was in, then Ailsa was probably somewhere near. She didn't have the nous to wander off. Too timid. Which was the main reason Steve married her.

He knocked on the door again. Saw a light come on in the hall. He looked over his shoulder at the road. Empty. Shug hoped that Len and Golly would take the hint and keep down. He didn't hear any sirens, either. Wondered if one or both of them had bled out.

The front door opened. He turned back to see Ailsa stood in the doorway, blinking at him. She was wearing going-out clothes, but looked dishevelled enough to have just come in. The smell that came off her was perfume and gin, reminded him of their mam. So did her voice, which was shaking when she said, "Shuggie?"

"Aye."

"Oh my God, Shug." She stepped out, threw loose arms around his neck and squeezed him. "I wasn't expecting to see you for ... I don't know. How long's it been?"

"A while."

Ailsa pulled back to have a look at him. "So what happened?"

"Nothing."

"How come's you're out early?" She took a sharp breath. "You didnae do anything daft, did you?"

"You know me, I did plenty daft. But no, Ails, I'm out properly."

"Really?"

"Uh-huh."

Punched him in the arm. Still had some strength in her. "Away with you."

"Serious."

A voice from behind her, braying up the hall. "Letting the bloody cold in, woman, who is it?"

Ailsa smiled. "You want to come in for a bit?"

"Aye."

She stepped back and let him into the warmth of the hall, closed the front door behind him. She nodded to the open door to the front room. Blue light flickered in there. Shug saw Steve laid out in his recliner, watching the highlights.

Steve said, "Well, who the bloody hell was it? This time of night, I hope you told them where to get off."

"Aye, she did."

Steve turned sharply in the recliner, made the springs screech. He was a big man but, as the line goes, out of shape. Money-soft and none the better for it. Kind of bloke whose missus had to stay half-pissed to deal with his moods, with the occasional battering. And judging by the way the light danced across the scabs on his right hand, he'd been at it recently. But Shug didn't want to dwell on that. Already lost it once tonight, and he could justify it as self-defence. Beating fuck out of Steve would just be indulgent, no matter how much the bastard deserved it.

"Shug," said Steve. "How you doing? You okay?"

"Not bad."

Steve kicked the footrest down. "Can I get you a drink or something? Ailsa, get your brother a beer."

"You want a Stella?" said Ailsa.

"No." Shug turned to his sister. "Fi said she gave you something to hold onto for us."

Ailsa looked at Steve.

Shug said, "What you looking at him for?"

"Yeah, what you looking at me for?" Steve laughed. "You know what he's talking about. Go and get it."

"Sorry, Shug."

Ailsa left the room before Shug got a chance to ask her why. He heard her run up the stairs as he turned to Steve, who was busy shifting his weight from one socked foot to the other. He looked at the television.

"That new, is it?" he said.

"That? Nah, had it for ages."

"Looks pricey."

"Nah."

"HD job."

"It's all HD now, Shug."

"Seeing a lot of them about, right enough." Shug pulled out his pack of cigarettes. Didn't bother asking if he could smoke. Didn't need to. He sparked the lighter, puffed smoke and moved his head at the television. "So if I get what I came for and I find that some of it's gone, you'll just, what, you'll shrug at us, will you?"

"I don't know what you're talking about."

Course he didn't. That was why he couldn't keep still. That was why he looked guilty as fuck. "I'm talking about a brand new telly, Steve. Looks to me like it might've cost upwards of a grand. Believe me, I'm getting to be quite the fuckin' expert on tellies tonight, so I know stuff like this. And unless I'm very much mistaken, that's upwards of a grand that you don't have. Or at least you didn't have until Ailsa brought in my stash to look after."

Steve was shaking his head, his mouth open. Smiling, like he was trying to come up with a decent excuse but his brain wasn't working, so he just looked like he was having a mild stroke.

"What'd you think, like, it was a bank up there? Take an interest-free loan, and you've got seven years to pay it back?"

Steve stopped moving his head now, his gaze stuck to the carpet. He breathed out through his mouth. Ailsa came down the stairs, slower than she'd gone up them. Shug heard her come into the room.

"Shug —"

"Do us a favour and turn on the big light, will you?"

"It's all there."

"Come on, love, you know better than that."

Shug held out his hand. Ailsa gave it to him, then turned on the main light. She gasped at the sight of him, blood splattered all up his T-shirt.

"Shuggie —"

"It's alright," he said. Didn't know whether

that was Len or Golly. Didn't really matter either way. Might be adding to it soon. There was supposed to be eight grand and change in the box, but there didn't look to be more than five. He removed the money, saw his passport and his Granda's watch, the gold one they gave him the day he left the mine. Shug tucked the cash into the back pocket of his jeans, the passport into his jacket, and slipped the watch over the knuckles and onto his right wrist. He looked back at Ailsa. "I'll need a new shirt."

"I'll get you one." Ailsa left the room.

Steve frowned. "Wait a second —"

"Steve," said Shug. "I'm going to need the keys to the Land Rover an' all."

Looking him in the eyes now. "I already told you I never took your money."

"I know what you told us."

"Your girlfriend had it before —"

"I know. Could've been you. Could've been her. Could've been both, but it doesn't really matter. Not like it changes the situation. You're still going to give me the keys to your car."

"No, I'm not." He backed away a step, second-guessing himself. "Why?"

"Because if you don't, I'll shoot you in the face." Shug pulled the pistol, held it loose against one leg.

"I swear, we never took any money from you."

"I'm past caring. Thing is, I'm robbing you, Steve, because if I don't, I'm going to have to hurt you. Badly. Because you're a fat cunt who's belted my little sister for far too many years without someone showing you your fuckin' guts. And the only reason I don't do both is because I don't want to see the look on her face when she finds you in a bloody heap, and because I made myself a promise that I wouldn't seriously maim anyone else tonight. But here's the thing, Steve, I will do both if you continue to fuck me about."

Steve trembled, but his face was stone. "How dare you."

Shug blinked. "Eh?"

"How dare you come into my house and threaten me."

"Dinnae get blustery, Steve. Start crying or something, whatever you need, but dinnae come the fuckin' bolsh. It doesn't suit you and it'll get you nowhere." Shug readjusted his grip on the pistol. "I'm taking the car. The only choice you have is whether you get to keep your kneecaps, or whether I add one more to the tally."

Ailsa returned to the front room. Shug heard her stop dead in the corner of the room.

"What's going on?" she said.

"Your husband's about to make a very important decision. Way it's going, you might not want to be in the room when he makes it."

"Jesus, what's that? Is that a gun? Did you bring a gun into my house?"

"Yes."

"Shuggie —"

"Won't take a second. Steve?"

Steve looked at his wife, then dug around in his pocket. He pulled out his keys and gave them to Shug.

"Thank you." Shug replaced the pistol, pocketed the keys and held out one hand for the shirt Ailsa had brought. "Ta."

She slapped him hard on the chest. "Fuck d'you think you're doing?"

"Don't."

"Bringing a *gun* into the house."

"I'm going."

She was made up, but the light in here made Shug see through it, made him see the swelling on one side of her face. He put one hand on her cheek. His throat was dry. Needed saving, but never wanted it, and he was past asking.

"Is that it?" she said. "Flying visit?"

"Let him go," said Steve.

"Take care of yourself," Shug told Ailsa. "I'll be in touch once I'm settled, alright?"

He kissed her on the cheek and then moved past her into the hall and out of the house. Left Steve to reach for the phone, get on with calling the police. It was the logical next step for a man stripped of his motor and his dignity.

Shug approached the car, bleeped off the alarm.

He saw a figure approach out the corner of his eye, heard footsteps rattling up the pavement. He turned, reached back for the pistol at the same time.

Fiona.

He let go of the gun.

"Wait," she said.

He didn't want to. He couldn't. He had places to get to.

But he waited all the same.

9.

"Where you going?" she said.

Her eyes were wet. She'd approached slowly, warily. Like she wasn't sure how he'd react to her presence. He didn't know himself. Not yet. Didn't know why she was here. Found himself staring at her so long, she'd had to repeat the question.

"Away," he said.

"Where's that?"

He thought about telling her. Wondered how it would play. Decided he couldn't take the chance. "I'm not daft. You'll call the police."

She shook her head. "I wouldn't do that."

"Did it the last time."

She looked hurt. "When?"

"Time that got us put in."

"No, I didn't."

"I'm not daft." He attempted a smile; it felt wrong, his cheeks aching. "I ken what's been going on. You and Len."

She blinked at him, her mouth open. Lost for words.

"Or you and Golly. Doesn't matter which one, really. The bairn looks more like Len, mind." He sniffed. "Guessing he's the one behind the telly and the new furniture. He's the one been keeping you company while I was away. Because I'll tell you this, sure as fuckin' day, he's the one got us sent down. You might've made the call, Fi, but he's the one that really did it."

"It wasn't me. And the bairn —"

"I don't care. I sorted it."

"You what?"

"Pegged your boyfriend." He held up a finger. "Just the once. I'm not an animal. And it was self-defence. Coming at us with this." Shug showed the gun. Fiona moved away from him. "So I did what I had to do. Doesn't mean I didn't enjoy it, like."

"I thought you were different now," she said.

"I am."

"You just —"

"I wasn't angry. No emotion in it. It was just something that had to be done, and it's not like I went looking for it. They wouldn't have let us out of there alive." He looked back at the house. Ailsa had left them alone. "Anyway, I don't have much time, so what did you want?"

"I want you to stay."

"Can't."

"Why not?"

"I've got plans."

"What about us?"

"Four years gone, I didn't expect you to keep yourself to yourself, Fi. Thought we sorted all that the last time we talked. You said you didn't want to carry on with me in prison my whole fuckin' life, and I telt you then that I didn't have much fuckin' choice in the matter."

She shook her head, looked at the ground. Put one hand up to her eyes. "You haven't been taking your meds, have you?"

"What fuckin' meds?"

"You haven't been taking them. You should take them."

"I'm not on any fuckin' meds."

"You don't take them, they'll recall you. You know that."

"I need to go," he said.

"Shug —"

"Called the polis on us already, Fiona. I need to go."

"What for?"

Shug nodded at the car.

"No, Shug, come on."

He tapped his head. "I've got to keep the goal

in mind, Fi. If I don't then I'll lose it, and if I lose it I don't know what's going to happen."

She started crying. He didn't move. Didn't trust himself.

"Listen, I can't stay here. I pegged your boyfriend, remember? Got into a ruckus with Golly an' all. They'll want us to ..." He shook his head. "I can't stay."

He wanted to apologise. He didn't. Knew it was just the sight of her crying that made him want to do it.

"Why are you doing this?" she said.

"I don't get you."

She looked up. "You know he's yours. Jamie. The bairn. He's your bairn."

"I was away."

"And he's three, almost four."

Shug thought about it, tried to work out the maths. He wasn't sure. He couldn't get the numbers to add up right. He frowned, started to get confused. There was a dull, painful throb in the back of his eyes. When she came a little closer, he moved back towards the Land Rover.

"Whatever it is, Shug, we can deal with it. Whatever it is, you don't have to run. You know they'll catch you if you do. They'll catch you and they'll put you back in prison, and what am I going to do then?"

He shook his head, but he didn't look at her.

Same as it always was — soon as she didn't want him to do something, she muddled stuff up to confuse him into agreeing with her. He'd been through it over and over in his head all the time he was inside, especially after that last fight in the visiting room. Her talking about commitment, him asking her what the fuck he was supposed to do about it when he was locked up. And she'd pressed the point, one hand on her gut like she needed a shit, until he lost his temper. Her fault. She had this way of mincing his head up when she wanted to, and he couldn't let her do it to him again. Not when he was so close to getting out of here.

He moved back against the Land Rover. She put a hand on the bonnet.

"What do you think I've been doing all this time, Shug?"

"Don't know," he said.

"I've been waiting. That's what I've been doing. I've been waiting for you. I've been working hard to make a nice home for you to come back to so you can be well again. And I see you for five seconds and all you can talk about is your stash. Next thing I know you're off and I don't get a chance to say anything."

"You told Len I was there."

"Because he told me to. I was scared."

"Of him?"

"Of you. The way you were acting. Thought maybe he could come round and you'd see one of your old mates, and you'd calm down a bit."

He flashed on the old days: Shug steaming drunk, wound up, lashing out at Fiona.

"Didn't work," he said.

"He told us to tell him as soon as you got out."

"Aye, he's a paranoid fucker." He wiped his nose, nodded at her. "I need to go."

"Shug."

"Away from the car."

"You not going to talk to me?"

"Just did."

"Shug —"

Kept his voice low, but the intent clear: "Get away from the fuckin' car."

Silence between the pair of them. Shug didn't catch Fiona's eye, stared at her midriff instead. Wanted to smack her. The only thing stopping him was the tremble in his hands.

"You made up your mind, then."

"I promised myself," said Shug.

"And that's you set." Her voice cracked: "Okay."

She moved out of the way and Shug got into the Land Rover, pulled the door quickly shut behind him. She stepped out of the way, just managed to keep her fingers. Shug stared at the steering wheel. He could feel her watching him as he fumbled with the keys. Something hurt his throat, made the tremble worse. He ran one hand under his nose and sniffed back something wet.

Fiona was talking to him from behind the glass. A soft, pleading tone, but he couldn't make out what she was saying.

It was for the best. He'd made himself a promise that he wouldn't get distracted from the long-term goal. And so far he'd done well to keep that promise, despite what had happened. He sniffed and told himself the only thing he needed to do now was get the engine going, put the car in gear and drive off without looking at Fiona. If he could do that, the rest would be a piece of piss.

He turned the key in the ignition. The engine growled.

He saw her moving slightly in his peripheral vision. He put the car into gear.

Fiona said, "Please." And it sounded as if she was in the car with him.

His hands went loose on the steering wheel.

"Fuck off," he said, his voice thick.

And then he leaned on the accelerator, wrenched the steering wheel to one side, and lurched the Land Rover out of Ailsa and Steve's drive, leaving Fiona far behind.

10.

On the road, it was easier. He had room to breathe, time to think.

First thing he decided was: he wasn't going east. Too many people back in California with phones and fingers — the police would already have the car description and registration. So he had to think they were already way ahead of him, and they would expect him to go east, straight to the airport. So he wasn't going east.

South was out of the question, too. That was England, and too much to fucking deal with. There wasn't much point in heading across to Glasgow either. If anything, he'd rather deal with East Lothian police than fucking Lanarkshire. You couldn't trust the fucking weegies as far as you could piss them.

So: north. Into the wilds, the scenic route up through to Inverness, a straight shot and the last chance to see his homeland before skipping the ocean like a stone.

That was the plan. But the car had a thirst for diesel that meant Shug got as far as Bannockburn services before he had to stop. That was fine, though, because by that time, his gut thought his throat had been cut.

Shug parked the car and changed into Steve's shirt. Then he bought a Ginsters egg and bacon, a bag of cheese and onion McCoys, a king-size Snickers, and washed it all down with a big can of Red Bull. Something the matter with the pop, though, because he was still bone-shattered, something cracking under his muscles every time he tried to move. He couldn't drive until the caffeine kicked in, so he walked around the services until the Napa Valley caught him unawares.

There it was, a huge cardboard vista in the window of WH Smiths.

... and the wine is bottled poetry ...

Red vines. In the distance, a mountain shimmered in a heat haze. Above it, the bluest sky he'd ever seen. There were more than seven hundred wineries dealing with the kind of grapes, just saying their names made you sound posh and French and sophisticated: Pinot Noir, Chardonnay, Merlot, Cabernet Sauvignon ...

It was some advert for a travel guide that came free with a paper Shug would never read otherwise, but it sang to him. It told him that his dreams were closer than ever, reminded him that all this shite so far had been absolutely worth it. All he had to do was pick up some more clothes at the airport, as well as some luggage to put them in. He also had to remember to buy a return ticket else they'd have in him a windowless room all bastard night.

The Red Bull had started its growl. He breathed out through his nose.

Only other thing he needed was that guide. After all, it was fate, wasn't it? The paper could've done anywhere in the world, but they'd picked his dream as theirs.

Shug approached the gated window, looked at the seal that ran around it. Alarmed, probably. Daft to think otherwise. He looked down at the pile of papers under the cardboard advert, the pile of travel guides next to it, then turned around to see if there was anything big enough and heavy enough. There were bins and benches, but they all looked bolted to the floor. Again, daft to think they wouldn't be. Places like this, they were security conscious. Wasn't some post office in Bathgate, was it?

Shug pulled the pistol from the back of his jeans. He checked around, but there was nobody walking around in here apart from him. He hefted the gun in his hand, then approached the window again. Ran through the motions in his head first, timing it, the muscles in his hand and arm micro-twitching in their rehearsal.

Then he put the butt of the pistol through the window. Glass rained onto his feet. He knocked shards away, pushed his arm through the hole up to the pit and grabbed one of the travel guides. Then he backed quickly off from the window and walked briskly back towards the entrance to the services, the alarm screeching behind him.

It was cold outside. He breathed deep, slowed down. He looked for the Land Rover.

Saw the police car idling next to it.

Shug kept walking, didn't break stride. He tucked the travel guide into his jacket pocket, closed it up just in case the wind revealed the pistol in the small of his back. He walked the long way round the car park, kept an eye on the police car. He thought he saw two of them in there, both of them big enough to pose a threat. One of them was busy writing something down.

There were choices here. One of which was lose his fucking mind, which was the one that didn't so much appeal as demand to be done, especially when the police car moved towards him. Shug stopped at a Cavalier, turned his back on the police. He pretended to fumble around in his pocket for his car keys, then glanced down at the driver's side window.

Saw the elderly man staring at him. A split-second, and Shug thought it was Charlie, but then the man's face changed into a stranger's and started shouting at him from behind the glass. Shug stepped back as the man wound his window down.

"What d'you think you're playing at?" shouted the man.

Shug looked over his shoulder. The police car was up the other end of the car park, moving slowly. Then the brake lights flared. The car came to a stop.

"Get out of the car," said Shug.

"You what?"

Shug lunged through the open window, grabbed the old man round the neck and tried to pull him out. The man screamed for help. Shug reached for the pistol, brought it up under the man's quivering chins. The driver's door opened easily and the man stopped screaming, moving quickly out of the Cavalier and quietly begging to keep what little life he had left. Once the old man was both feet on the ground, Shug shoved him out of the way and moved to the driver's seat.

He looked up, saw one of the uniforms running towards him. Saw the police car already turned and pointed his way. He pulled the driver's door shut and stamped on the accelerator. The engine roared and then choked, the Cavalier rolling forwards on a stall. Shug saw the police car turn up ahead, bearing down on him from the front, blocking him off. He put the Cavalier into reverse, suddenly aware of the small noises he was making in the back of his throat.

The engine coughed again, didn't catch. The Cavalier rolled.

The driver's door flew open. The uniform put hands on him. Shug let go of the steering wheel, tried to scramble over the gear stick. The uniform grabbed a hold of Shug's jeans, yanked him back. Shug kicked out, screamed at the copper and twisted round to reach for his gun. Touched bare back instead.

Shug felt himself dragged out of the Cavalier. He saw the other uniform get out of the police car just before he was shoved against the side of the car. He looked down, saw the pistol at his feet but had no way of going for it. The pressure against his back was immense.

"Watch it with this one," said the car copper. "He's supposed to be a heid-the-ball."

"You mental?" said the uniform, grabbing one of Shug's wrists.

"Course he is. You only need to look at him."

Shug stared at the copper who'd been driving,

and then over his shoulder at the police car that stood with the driver's door hanging open and the engine running. He was tired, but he couldn't give up. Not now. He hung his head, felt the steel close around one wrist. Anticipated the uniform coming in for the other hand, and brought his foot down the uniform's shin to his instep, felt a satisfying crunch as his heel ground bone and then twisted out from the copper's grip.

Shug feinted to the left, ran right, vaulted the Cavalier's bonnet and made for the police car.

He shoved at the other copper, but felt his hand catch on something, his body carrying on regardless. Then pain flared in his wrist, something kicked him in the back and the ground reared up to kiss him. He fell hard, the kick turned to solid weight between his shoulder blades and his arm pulled back across his arse. Shug saw the world through fireworks and kicked out, screaming.

"Told you he was a fuckin' headcase."

"Hold him. Hold the fucker."

Shug threw himself around, felt the coppers struggle to keep a hold of him.

"Take the bastard's legs, Bri. He's a kicker, this one."

Too right. Shug showed them what kind of kicker he was. He lashed out with both feet, screaming until his head felt like it was ready to explode.

Then a whip across the backs of his legs. Once. Twice. He yelled with the pain, scrambled up to his knees for a second before another blow brought him crashing to his stomach. Something shifted from his jacket, a weight lost.

"*Got* the bastard."

His other arm, pulled up and clicked at the wrist. Something scraped against the tarmac. The Ginsters clawed its way up his throat, but he swallowed it back. He wasn't going to spew for these two. He tried to kick out again, but the message didn't reach his legs.

And then he saw the travel guide. It lay open on the tarmac, pages fluttering in the wind. He thought he saw the picture again, the one of the vineyard, and he stared at it, tried to brand it into his memory.

But there was Fiona with tears in her eyes. There was Len and Golly and blood on the lino. There was Ailsa with booze on her breath and a bruise on her cheek. He saw all of this, and the Napa Valley struggled to take, wouldn't stay in his head long enough to focus on. The pages blew over, back and forth, and soon the image fractured into a million pieces, leaving nothing behind.

Shug felt the blood go from his arms. The

floor lurched away from him as the coppers brought him to his feet. His dead legs buckled under his weight, the two uniforms holding him up. The copper who'd brought him to the deck moaned about the state of his trousers. The other copper leaned in nice and close and whispered a dull threat of revenge.

Shug didn't hear him. He stared at the travel guide, willing the image back into his head. He was still looking at it when they shoved him into the back of the police car.

But he still couldn't remember what California looked like.

Crime Express is an imprint of Five
Leaves Publications

www.fiveleaves.co.uk

Other titles include

Trouble in Mind by *John Harvey**
Claws by *Stephen Booth*
The Mentalist by *Rod Duncan**
The Quarry by *Clare Littleford**
The Okinawa Dragon by *Nicola Monaghan**
Gun by *Ray Banks**
Killing Mum by *Allan Guthrie**
Not Safe by *Danuta Reah*
Graven Image by *Charlie Williams*

* A6 format, with French flaps